To all my fans, thank you for enabling me to do what I do. I appreciate ALL of you. <3

-Ms Naughtee

Join me on my FREE Substack for exclusive pictures, additional stories/sex scenes, and more!

https://msnaughtee.substack.com/

CONTENTS

Dedication
Chapter 1: Holidays Approaching   2
Chapter 2: Party Planning   6
Chapter 3: The Night Of   10
Chapter 4: Socializing   14
Chapter 5: The Proposal   18
Chapter 6: It Begins   23
Chapter 7: Play Time   25
Chapter 8: One More Go   30
Chapter 9: Cleaning Up   33
Books By This Author   38

Gangbang: By The Christmas Tree

MS Naughtee

CHAPTER 1: HOLIDAYS APPROACHING

The glow of twinkling fairy lights filled Tessa and Kieran's home, casting a golden warmth over the cozy space. Outside, the first snowflakes of December drifted down in lazy spirals, blanketing the yard and tracing soft white lines on the windowpanes. Inside, the scent of freshly baked gingerbread lingered in the air, mingling with the piney aroma of their towering Christmas tree, which they had decorated just last weekend. Tessa moved around the kitchen in thick socks and an oversized, off-the-shoulder sweater, humming a carol under her breath as she put the finishing touches on a tray of cookies.

Kieran sat nearby, reclined at the kitchen counter, his eyes sparkling as he watched her work. "You're spoiling me, you know," he teased, reaching over to snag a cookie. She gave him a playful swat on the hand, but the smile on her face was unmistakable.

"Those aren't for you! Not yet, anyway," she chided, grinning as he pretended to look heartbroken. "They're for the party."

He let out a dramatic sigh. "But the party is days away! You can't just taunt a man with gingerbread and expect him to hold out!"

Tessa rolled her eyes, stepping over to kiss him on the cheek. "Fine, you can have one. Just one."

He didn't need to be told twice. Taking a bite, he let out an exaggerated groan. "Perfect, as usual. Remind me again why we're hosting this party if it means sharing your baked masterpieces with other people? Why would I ever agree to that?" He teased her with a playful smirk on his face.

She laughed, the sound filling the house and mixing with the soft hum of Christmas music in the background. "Because we love our friends, and because you promised me we'd do it every year. Plus, you know they're looking forward to it as much as we are."

Kieran sighed, pretending to consider her words, then broke into a grin. "All right, I'll allow it," he teased. "But only because I enjoy hearing everyone rave about your cooking."

They exchanged a lingering look, both of them feeling the holiday spirit settle over them like a warm blanket. There was something magical about this time of year—something that made even the smallest gestures feel meaningful.

"So, are you ready for Friday?" she asked, leaning against the counter and twirling a strand of hair between her fingers.

"Ready to see Jackson try to flirt with every woman in the room? Ready to hear Lily's awful but somehow adorable karaoke rendition of 'All I Want for Christmas'? You bet," Kieran chuckled. "You know, it might just be our best party yet."

She smirked, raising a brow. "Oh, is that right? What makes you say that?"

"Well, we've never missed a year, and each one keeps getting wilder." He gave her a sly look. "And something tells me you might have a few surprises up your sleeve."

Tessa feigned innocence, brushing a strand of hair from her face as she turned to pour them both glasses of wine. "Surprises? I don't know what you're talking about," she said, handing him a glass.

They clinked their glasses together, the soft chime lingering in the room. "To our little tradition," he said, meeting her gaze.

"And to a Christmas season we won't forget," she replied, her eyes twinkling.

They both took a sip, letting the warmth of the wine settle into their bodies. The lights from the tree reflected in Tessa's eyes, and for a moment, Kieran felt like the luckiest man in the world. Moments like these reminded him of how much he loved their life together—simple yet rich, filled with laughter, and, occasionally, a bit of spice.

"So," he said, leaning back, "are we going all out with the decorations again?"

Tessa nodded. "We have to! Every year it's a little bit extra. Besides, it's the one time of year we get everyone together."

"True. Although I think we're going to need a bigger space soon if we keep adding people to the guest list." He looked around, as if their kitchen might somehow expand to accommodate everyone they'd invited.

She laughed, picturing their friends squeezed into the cozy house. "A packed house, a roaring fire, and all our favourite people...sounds perfect to me."

"Me too," he said softly. "And you know, I do love our tradition of everyone letting loose." He leaned in, his voice lowering. "Especially you." He couldn't help but lean in to kiss her again. Tessa happily kissed him back.

She felt her cheeks warm under his gaze, but she gave him a coy smile. "Well, if you're lucky, I might have a little something special planned just for you this year."

Kieran raised an eyebrow, his curiosity piqued. "Now, that's the kind of holiday spirit I'm talking about."

They laughed, clinking their glasses again as they imagined the fun, mischief, and laughter that awaited them and their friends. The season had just begun, and the best was yet to come.

CHAPTER 2: PARTY PLANNING

Tessa was sprawled on the couch, notepad and pen in hand, as she and Kieran discussed the details for their upcoming Christmas party. She tapped her pen thoughtfully, glancing up at him with a mischievous smile. "So, we've got the gingerbread, and a whole tray of sugar cookies… but I feel like we need something else. Something rich and decadent."

Kieran was on the other end of the couch, scrolling through recipes on his phone, nodding in agreement. "Definitely. Maybe a big batch of brownies or something with peppermint? Something people can snack on after they've had a few drinks." He gave her a wink, clearly anticipating the lively night ahead.

"Good idea. And speaking of drinks, we need eggnog—both the spiked and non-spiked versions, right?" She jotted it down, along with a few flavours she thought their friends would enjoy. "And maybe a couple of bottles of rum to add to it?"

"Definitely rum. And we should probably get some bourbon for those who prefer it a little classier," Kieran suggested. "Plus, wine and maybe a couple of holiday cocktails? We could try that cranberry-orange spritzer recipe I saw last week."

Tessa nodded, her excitement growing as the list of party essentials grew. "Let's add whiskey and a good gin to the list, too. You know Jackson always brings his fancy cocktail shaker and tries to out-mix everyone else."

Kieran laughed, picturing their friend's elaborate cocktail-making routine. "I think he even brings his own bitters sometimes. It wouldn't be a party without Jackson showing off behind the bar. What an idiot."

They both laughed, exchanging stories of their friends' holiday quirks, envisioning the lively gathering that was only days away. Tessa, chewing on the end of her pen, leaned back and stretched her legs across Kieran's lap, a thoughtful expression on her face.

"There is…one other thing I've been thinking about," she started, her voice softening, and Kieran glanced over with a curious smile.

"Okay," he replied, setting his phone down to give her his full attention. "What's on your mind?"

Tessa hesitated for a moment, gathering her thoughts. "Remember when we talked a while back about, you know, our little fantasy?"

Kieran had a questioning look about him. "Which one?" He asked, wanting to be certain.

"You know the one," Tessa told him, a little surprised he hadn't immediately figured it out.

Kieran's eyebrows lifted slightly, and he grinned knowingly. "You mean the one involving… more people?"

She smiled, looking slightly bashful but also clearly excited. "Yes, that one. I was just thinking…maybe this could be the right time to try it out? It could just be a couple of friends, people we trust…if you're open to it."

Kieran's gaze held hers, his expression equal parts intrigued and thoughtful. "Well, I'm definitely open to it," he said, his voice low. "But let's talk through it. I want to make sure we're both comfortable with everything—what we'd be okay with, what we wouldn't be. Boundaries and all that."

Tessa nodded, relieved and encouraged by his response. "Absolutely. I'd want us both to feel completely safe and in control the entire time. And I want us to decide together who we'd invite, if we even go through with it."

Kieran reached out, brushing a strand of hair from her face. "You know I'd be into it, but it means everything to me that you're comfortable. Let's go over everything so that there are no surprises."

They spent the next few minutes talking through their boundaries, each sharing their own thoughts and limits with care and honesty. Both of them emphasized that the focus was on respect and mutual enjoyment, ensuring that every step of the experience would be consensual and understood by all involved. They agreed that communication would be key and that they'd only take things as far as they both felt comfortable.

The pair also made it clear, this wasn't meant to take over the entire party. They still wanted to keep all their friends. They wanted to be able to have their normal, drunken Christmas parties going forward. They just thought they could invite a few of their more, shall we say, adventurous friends, to join them in their activities if they were still around towards the end of the night.

The two continued to discuss and dissect how they should be sure not to ruin the party, hurt anyone's feelings, or most importantly: harm their relationship. These were the key goals. If any of them were looking like they'd be broken or violated, the couple agreed to abort the mission.

When they finally wrapped up their conversation, Tessa felt a warmth in her chest—not just from the excitement of their plan, but from the deep trust and understanding she and Kieran shared. She leaned over, planting a soft kiss on his lips.

"You make everything feel right," she murmured. She

looked overly pleased with herself, and Kieran as well.

Kieran smiled, pulling her close. "That's because we do it together. As long as we're together, it'll be fun! Now, let's finish planning the best Christmas party yet."

The two resumed kissing, this time more passionately. Perhaps it was the wine, or their love for one another. But more than likely, this makeout session was spurred on by the excitement for their upcoming fuckfest.

With their list complete and their plans taking shape, the night carried on with laughter, closeness, and a renewed anticipation for the days ahead.

CHAPTER 3: THE NIGHT OF

Tessa glanced at herself in the hallway mirror, making a final adjustment to her dark green velvet dress. It hugged her curves just right, falling to mid-thigh, with a subtle, daring neckline that made her feel both festive and alluring. She swept a hand through her long brunette waves, adding a bit of gloss to her lips before stepping back to survey the whole look. Just as she turned, she saw Kieran entering the room, dressed in a sharp black shirt, dark jeans, and the hint of a smirk that always got her heart racing.

His eyes swept over her, lingering in appreciation. "Well, I think it's safe to say this is going to be the best-looking Christmas party yet," he murmured, pulling her into a gentle embrace.

Tessa grinned, resting her hands on his chest as she tilted her head up to meet his gaze. "And I think you're just saying that because you're biased," she teased.

"Maybe," he replied with a wink, "but I'm still right." Leaning down, he captured her lips in a slow, lingering kiss that made her feel warm from head to toe.

They held each other close for a moment, savouring the quiet before the chaos of the night began. Tessa couldn't help but smile, feeling the excitement building. "I love you," she whispered, brushing her fingers along his jawline.

"I love you, too," he replied, his voice soft but filled with that unmissable edge of anticipation. "Let's make this the best Christmas party yet."

Just then, the doorbell rang, signaling the arrival of their first guests. They shared a last quick kiss and a grin before pulling themselves apart. Kieran gave her one more admiring look as he walked to the door, and Tessa took a deep breath, letting the buzz of excitement settle into her bones.

As Kieran opened the door, they were greeted by the bright, laughing faces of their friends, bundled up in scarves and coats, cheeks pink from the cold. They burst into the house with a flurry of hugs and "Merry Christmas!" greetings, shedding their layers and gathering around the warmly lit living room, which had been decorated with red ribbons, sparkling garlands, and an impressively tall Christmas tree that glittered with silver and gold ornaments.

"Your place looks amazing!" Their friend Lily exclaimed, eyeing the decor as she handed Tessa a bottle of wine. "Every year, it feels like it just gets more magical in here."

Tessa laughed, accepting the wine. "Thanks, Lil! We're trying to outdo ourselves this year." She smiled as she walked with Lily further into her home. A few other friends trailed behind.

In the kitchen, Kieran poured out the first round of drinks, popping open a bottle of wine and setting out some holiday-themed glasses. Soon, Jackson arrived with his signature cocktail shaker and a bag of mysterious mixers, as promised. Kieran and Tessa made eye contact with one another from across the room. They couldn't help but giggle.

"Time to get festive, everyone!" Jackson declared, shaking up a cocktail for anyone who dared try his experimental holiday concoction. As friends milled about the kitchen and living room, Tessa and Kieran exchanged glances, amused by the familiar antics unfolding.

Tessa moved around the room, catching up with each of her friends. Everywhere she looked, there were people laughing, clinking glasses, and embracing the spirit of the night. She could already tell it was going to be one of those evenings filled with warmth and laughter—one that they'd remember for years to come.

At one point, Kieran wrapped an arm around her from behind, handing her a drink as they watched the room fill with happy chatter and festive cheer. "We did good," he murmured in her ear, pressing a quick kiss to her temple.

"Yeah, we did," she agreed, leaning into him with a contented sigh. "This is perfect." Tessa was so pleased things seemed to be going exactly as she'd envisioned.

As the night continued, the living room came alive with stories from the past year, shared jokes, and that familiar joy of friends gathering to celebrate. It had been a long time since they'd seen a few of their friends. This chance to catch up was appreciated by all.

Jackson had set up his own little cocktail station by the kitchen island, offering his creations to anyone willing to try them, which usually came with a flair of drama and showmanship that only he could pull off. Meanwhile, others were diving into the trays of Tessa's cookies and gingerbread, already claiming them as "the best yet."

Soon enough, Christmas music began to play, and a spontaneous dance party broke out, with some friends taking turns leading their own renditions of Christmas classics. Lily, as always, was the first to grab a spoon as a makeshift microphone, belting out a joyful but hilariously off-key version of "All I Want for Christmas Is You." She was no Mariah Carey.

Between the clinking glasses, warm embraces, and joyous laughter that filled every corner of the room, the party had truly begun. Tessa and Kieran moved through the crowd hand in hand, stealing kisses when they thought no one was watching, revelling in the warmth of the holiday and the love they felt for each other.

And as the evening carried on, with the snow falling gently outside, Tessa knew this was exactly how she'd imagined it— surrounded by good friends, wrapped in the magic of Christmas, and beside the man who made everything feel complete.

CHAPTER 4: SOCIALIZING

The party was in full swing. Tessa drifted through the lively crowd, a glass of red wine in hand, stopping to chat and laugh with old friends and new acquaintances who'd come to join the festive night. Across the room, Kieran stood by the bar, sipping from a glass of spiked eggnog and keeping an eye on the night as it unfolded. Every so often, he'd catch Tessa's eye, and they'd exchange a smile, a little silent check-in that reminded her he was close by, enjoying the party with her.

Near the kitchen, she spotted her longtime friend Lily, her arms full of holiday treats she'd been sharing with everyone. Lily was a petite woman with a bubbly energy that lit up any room she walked into, her laughter infectious and her stories endless.

"Tessa!" Lily called out, making her way over. "Okay, I have to ask, did you make the brownies? I swear they're better than last year's."

Tessa laughed, holding her hands up in mock defence. "Guilty as charged! But it's just the same recipe with a little extra peppermint."

"Well, whatever it is, I'm already three in, and I don't plan on stopping anytime soon." Lily nudged Tessa playfully, her cheeks rosy from the wine she'd been enjoying. "Also, can I just say that you and Kieran really outdid yourselves with the decorations this year? It's gorgeous."

"Thanks, Lily," Tessa replied, her gaze briefly scanning the room. "It's been so fun putting everything together. We really wanted to make it feel special."

"Oh, it does! I just love how cozy and festive everything is," Lily said, her gaze drifting over the glittering garlands and candle-lit corners of the room.

They chatted for a while about their plans for the holidays, comparing notes on gifts they'd picked out for their families, until a familiar voice called out from behind them.

"Ladies!" It was Jackson, arriving with his usual flourish, a cocktail shaker in hand and a grin on his face. He was tall and lean, with a knack for drawing attention, his enthusiasm impossible to resist. "Who's ready for the best holiday cocktails of the year?"

Tessa and Lily exchanged amused glances, and Tessa held up her wine glass. "I'm good, but I think Lily could use a refill!"

"Oh, come on!" Jackson teased, pouring Lily a drink. "One sip of this, and you'll forget all about your wine." He gave his shaker a few vigorous shakes, pouring out a vibrant cranberry cocktail and handing it to her with a wink.

Kieran appeared then, joining their little group with a casual arm around Tessa's shoulders. He took a sip of his eggnog, nodding at Jackson with a playful smile. "Showing off your bartending skills again, huh, Jackson?"

"Always, my friend," Jackson replied with a mock bow. "I live to please."

They laughed together, and as the conversation drifted to stories of past Christmas parties, Tessa's gaze caught sight of her friend Mike setting up a game of beer pong at the table in the corner.

"Oh, now we're talking!" Tessa said, nudging Kieran.

"Should we show them how it's done?"

Kieran chuckled, giving her shoulder a gentle squeeze. "You're on."

They joined Mike at the table, and soon a few more friends gathered around, laughing and cheering as Tessa and Kieran teamed up. Tessa lined up her first shot with exaggerated focus, balancing the ping pong ball on her fingertips. She squinted, made a show of her aim, and—much to everyone's surprise—landed it perfectly in one of the cups.

"Looks like Tessa's got her game face on tonight!" Mike laughed, raising his cup in mock surrender.

As the game went on, the teasing grew bolder, and the laughter only louder. Tessa and Kieran exchanged high-fives every time one of them landed a shot, the lighthearted competitiveness bringing out a playful side to their evening.

After a few rounds, Tessa slipped away to get a refill on her wine, catching her breath as she made her way back to the living room. She found herself beside an old friend, Ben, who she hadn't seen in ages. Ben was easygoing with a warm, easy smile, his dark hair cropped short and his eyes lighting up when he saw her approach.

"Tessa! It's been too long!" he greeted her, wrapping her in a quick hug.

"Ben! I'm so glad you made it," Tessa replied, her eyes bright with excitement. "It's been what, a couple of years?"

"Something like that. I've missed these parties," Ben said, glancing around at the festive scene. "Looks like you and Kieran really went all out."

They talked, reminiscing about past Christmases, and Ben filled her in on his travels and recent job change. Tessa listened intently, genuinely interested in his stories, while the sound of the party continued to hum around them.

"So, are you and Kieran still the life of the party?" Ben asked, a playful glint in his eyes.

Tessa laughed, glancing across the room to see Kieran chatting with Lily and a couple of other friends. "I don't know about 'life of the party,' but we try to make things fun. And… we have a few ideas for tonight," she said, raising an eyebrow playfully.

"Oh, I like the sound of that." Ben's smile turned just a bit more mischievous, his gaze lingering on hers for a beat. "You always did have the best ideas."

She felt her cheeks warm, a faint thrill stirring as they exchanged a look that lingered just a moment too long to be innocent. "Well, I'll be sure to let you know if you're needed for any of them," she replied, her tone light but with an unmistakable hint of flirtation.

Kieran caught sight of the two from across the room, watching as Tessa and Ben laughed together, their easy banter taking on a subtle, flirtatious edge. He didn't mind the way she laughed a little louder, her eyes bright as she and Ben exchanged stories and little compliments—it was all part of the fun, and he knew they were both enjoying the energy it brought to the night.

As the evening wore on, the party continued with laughter, clinking glasses, and friendly games, everyone caught up in the warmth and joy of the season. Tessa and Kieran made their way around the room together and apart, socializing with friends, sharing in the fun, and revelling in the lighthearted holiday spirit.

With the lights twinkling, music playing, and conversations flowing freely, they knew this would be a night to remember—a night of connections, celebration, and a little something extra just waiting to unfold.

CHAPTER 5: THE PROPOSAL

As the party buzzed around them, Tessa and Kieran found a quiet moment to steal away to a cozy nook by the living room fireplace. She nestled beside him, her cheeks flushed from both the wine and the little thrill of her conversation with Ben. Kieran leaned in, his hand gently resting on her knee, eyes dancing with curiosity.

"So, I noticed you and Ben were getting along pretty well," he began, his tone light but probing, a smile tugging at the corners of his lips. "Anything... interesting I should know about that chat?"

Tessa's eyes sparkled, and she took a small sip from her wine, letting his question hang in the air just a moment before answering. "You could say that. We were definitely flirting. But I think you already knew that."

Kieran chuckled, running his thumb in soft circles over her knee. "I could tell," he admitted, voice low and approving. "And I like it. Seeing you like that... It's kind of exciting."

They shared a knowing look, both enjoying the subtle current between them. Tessa placed her hand on his, fingers intertwining as they let the idea of their plan settle between them, comfortable and thrilling. She bit her lip, considering how to bring up the next part.

"So... about that idea we talked about," she started slowly, studying his face. "What if we made it a little... extra special?"

"Extra special?" Kieran raised an eyebrow, amused, but intrigued. He could only wonder where she was going with this.

"Yes," she continued, her voice soft and enticing. "I was thinking, what if we actually asked a few of our friends to join us later? Just a couple of the right people, people we trust..."

Kieran's eyes gleamed with interest, and he let out a small, appreciative hum. "You mean... tonight? I'm in if you are." This was exactly the answer Tessa wanted to hear.

They exchanged a shared grin, both of them leaning into the idea with growing excitement. "I was thinking maybe Ben," she offered, meeting his eyes to gauge his reaction.

"Ben... definitely." Kieran nodded in agreement. "And what about Jackson?" he suggested, a smile forming as he thought of their friend's easygoing charm. "He's been practically attached to that cocktail shaker all night."

Tessa laughed, nodding. "I was thinking the same. And... maybe Mike, too? He's been a friend for years, and I think he'd be open to it. Plus, we all know each other so well."

"I think we're all about to get to know each other *very* well," Kieran teased. Tessa couldn't help but giggle.

With their shortlist set, the two shared a charged, anticipatory silence, the weight of their decision thrilling and tantalizing. It was all falling into place perfectly.

"Okay," Kieran said, voice firm but playful, "let's see if they're up for it. We'll have to be discreet, but I think we can talk to them one by one."

They decided to start with Ben. Kieran spotted him refilling his drink near the bar and gave Tessa an encouraging nod. She sauntered over, slipping beside Ben, whose eyes lit up at her approach.

"Ben," she began, leaning close enough so only he could hear, "I wanted to ask you something... a little unusual." Her voice dropped just enough to add a touch of mystery, her eyes holding his in an inviting way.

"Oh?" Ben replied, looking intrigued, a smile tugging at his lips. "You've got my attention."

Tessa gave a small, playful smile, glancing around to make sure no one else could overhear. "So, Kieran and I... well, we were talking about you. And we wanted to see if you'd be open to joining us later. Something a bit... more private."

Ben's eyes widened slightly, surprise flashing across his face before giving way to an intrigued smile. "You're serious?" he asked, his tone laced with curiosity and excitement. He seemed to know precisely what she was asking.

"Very," she replied, her eyes sparkling. "But only if you're interested. We thought it could be something fun, no pressure."

After a moment of consideration, Ben nodded, a slow, pleased grin spreading across his face. "I'd definitely be interested," he replied, voice low and eager. "Just let me know when."

"Will do," Tessa responded. She gave his arm a light squeeze, smiling warmly before she slipped back to Kieran's side to give him a small nod, confirming their first invite.

Next was Jackson. Kieran made his way over to where Jackson was showing off a new cocktail creation to some of their friends. When Jackson spotted Kieran approaching, he grinned, holding up his glass. "Kieran! You've got to try this, man—it's my best one yet."

Kieran took a sip, giving an approving nod. "Pretty impressive," he said, leaning in slightly to lower his voice.

"Actually, I wanted to talk to you about something else too."

Jackson's curiosity piqued, and he raised an eyebrow. "Oh? What's up?"

Kieran kept his tone casual but direct. "Tessa and I were thinking of extending the evening in a... unique way. Just a few close friends. We wanted to know if you'd be interested in joining us for something a bit more intimate, later on."

For a moment, Jackson was silent, his surprise obvious. Kieran tried to discern if he detected a slight blush on Jackson's face, but he wasn't sure. Then a slow smile spread across his face as he caught on. "Well, well, well," he said, leaning back with a mischievous grin. "I'd be honoured to join you two. This sounds... exciting."

Kieran laughed, patting his friend on the shoulder. "I thought you'd be up for it. We'll give you a signal when things wind down." Jackson nodded understandingly.

With Jackson on board, there was only Mike left. Tessa and Kieran exchanged a look as they spotted him at the beer pong table. Tessa made her way over, greeting him with a friendly smile.

"Hey Mike, having fun?" she asked, watching as he took a shot, sinking the ball into a cup with a small cheer.

"Always," he replied with a grin, giving her a hug. "You guys really know how to throw a great party."

They chatted a bit, and as the conversation eased, Tessa leaned in, lowering her voice slightly. "Actually, there's something I wanted to ask you, Mike. Kieran and I were wondering if you'd like to join us later... just us, in a more private setting."

Mike looked at her, surprise flickering across his face before he broke into a broad smile. "You mean?..." he asked, his voice hushed with intrigue as he trailed off. From the look on Tessa's face, he began to understand she was serious. He could tell from her bright eyes and her flirty smirk that she meant every word.

"Completely," Tessa replied, giving him a playful, inviting smile. "But only if you're comfortable."

Mike nodded, looking both surprised and pleased. "Count me in," he replied, chuckling. "You two really know how to make a party unforgettable!"

With their invitations extended and their three friends in on the plan, Tessa and Kieran reunited by the fireplace, a thrill buzzing between them. They exchanged a soft, lingering kiss, the anticipation of the night filling the space between them.

"Looks like it's all set," Kieran murmured, brushing a strand of hair from her face.

Tessa nodded, her eyes filled with excitement. "I can't believe we're actually doing this," she whispered, her smile wide. "But I wouldn't want it any other way, not with anyone but you."

He wrapped his arms around her, pulling her close, the warmth of the fireplace mirroring the warmth between them. The two held each other tightly and engaged in a deep and loving kiss. The rest of the night was already set in motion, and they knew it would be one to remember.

CHAPTER 6: IT BEGINS

As the final guests gathered their coats and murmured sleepy farewells, Kieran and Tessa exchanged a knowing glance. The party's energy had mellowed, and a comfortable hush settled over the house as people left, waving goodbye with drowsy smiles. Only a handful remained—Ben, Jackson, and Mike—each lounging around, chatting in lowered voices as the night's quiet excitement began to take on a different feel.

Kieran gave Tessa a small nod, their shared plan sparking between them as she moved to the group, her eyes bright with invitation. "Well, gentlemen," she began softly, "are you still up for that... private gathering we mentioned?"

The three men exchanged glances, each one smiling with anticipation. With a warm, encouraging look from Kieran, Tessa led the way upstairs, feeling a thrill of anticipation. As they entered the bedroom, the lighting softened by the glow of flickering candles and dimmed lamps, the mood felt rich with promise. Kieran and Tessa had set the room carefully beforehand—plush pillows stacked on the bed, soft blankets folded at the foot, and a warmth that made the space feel intimate and inviting.

Once inside, Tessa moved to the centre of the room, turning to face her guests with a playful smile. She looked over at Kieran, who gave her an encouraging nod. Slowly, she began unbuttoning her blouse, her movements smooth and deliberate, her eyes never leaving theirs. She slipped it off her shoulders, letting it slide to the floor to reveal a lacy, deep-red bra that highlighted her figure beautifully.

The men watched, captivated, as she unzipped her skirt and let it fall around her ankles, stepping out of it with ease. She was left standing in her lingerie, the delicate fabric hugging her curves, and a quiet confidence radiating from her as she looked at each of them in turn. Her smile was warm and playful, and she noticed the appreciative, knowing glances they exchanged with one another.

Kieran stood beside her, reaching for her hand and giving it a gentle squeeze. The room pulsed with anticipation, the promise of what was to come hanging thick in the air. Tessa's eyes sparkled as she shared one last, playful look with Kieran before turning her attention to the men, who watched her with eager, yet respectful expressions.

"Ready, boys?" Tessa asked boldly with an underlying tone of sensuality. She sounded almost like a drill sergeant ready to whip them into shape.

Unequivocally, the men nodded. They looked eager. Like hungry dogs who'd just spotted their first meal in days.

With her heart racing and a sense of excitement coursing through her, Tessa gave them a coy smile, ready to take this night exactly where she and Kieran had dreamed. The men returned her look with grins of their own, nodding to each other, clearly ready to follow her lead into the night ahead.

Without even another word, everyone there knew. This was going to be *fun*.

CHAPTER 7: PLAY TIME

Tessa took a deep breath, her heart pounding with anticipation as she stepped closer to the men. She could feel Kieran's eyes on her, watching her every move, and it only made her wetter. She knew what was coming, and she couldn't wait.

Ben was the first to move, walking right over to touch Tessa immediately. His hands roamed her body as he pulled her closer. This only helped build Kieran's excitement.

Tessa moaned, giving into his touch, as she felt his fingers trailing over her smooth, soft skin. He leaned in, his lips brushing against her neck, as he whispered, "You're so fucking sexy, Tessa. I can't wait to have you."

Tessa moaned, staring at the other men as Ben felt her up. "Please," she whimpered. "Fuck me, boys. I want all of you to fuck me."

Ben grinned, his eyes filled with lust as he began to strip off his clothes, revealing his thin, muscular body. Tessa's eyes widened, her breath catching in her throat as she took in the sight of him. He was just the first guy to begin stripping, and already, she liked what she was seeing.

Jackson and Mike followed suit, stripping off their clothes to reveal themselves next. Each of them dropped their clothes to the floor, showing off their tattooed frames. Mike was more muscular than Jackson, as Jackson's build was a bit thinner and similar to Ben's.

Tessa loved the building anticipation. She moaned out, as

the other men moved over to touch her now. She was beginning to feel helpless. Just as she'd wanted. The strong, forceful men could do whatever they wanted with her. And there was little she could do about it. It was a fantasy of hers to serve multiple big, strong men at once.

Tessa felt her heart racing as Ben pushed her down onto the bed, his hands roaming over her body as he pulled her lingerie off, revealing her shaved, most intimate areas. She moaned, her hips moving against his touch, as he began to rub her wet little pussy.

She groaned as she stared directly up into Kieran's eyes. Her eyes alone signalled to him that she was ready for this. All of it.

Kieran stripped himself down too, wanting to be in on the fun. But he also knew how rare this opportunity was. He asked Tessa if he should get some pictures and film some of it for them to look back on later. She nodded her head rapidly. She wanted to be able to relive this fantasy forever.

Then, her attention was turned back to the men on the bed. Ben softly grabbed her face, tilting her by her chin so she looked toward him.

"You ready for me?" Ben asked, his voice low and rough. "You ready to get fucked like the naughty girl you are?"

Tessa sighed, her cravings only growing. "Yes," she gasped. "Fuck me, Ben. Fuck me hard."

Ben grinned, as he climbed aboard her in missionary and teased her little pussy lips with his large, stiff member. Tessa moaned again. He felt so big, so hard, and she knew she was going to get the fucking of her life. His cock was practically making her gush just resting atop her pussy. She could hardly wait to feel him stretching her, filling her right up.

The other boys watched with jealousy as Ben began to slowly slip inside. Tessa could do little but moan softly. Her fantasy was now beginning to take shape.

As Ben began to fuck her harder, his hips slamming against her ass with each deep thrust, Jackson and Mike positioned themselves on either side of her, their cocks rubbing against her smooth, soft skin. Tessa groaned as the men appeared beside her on the bed. She was surrounded by muscular men and big hard cocks. Like she'd always dreamt of.

Kieran was snapping pics rapidly, and couldn't resist the urge to stroke himself. It was such a hot scene. And it may have been something they'd experience just once in a lifetime. Tessa looked at him and was certain he liked it. She watched as he tugged on his cock and she hoped he was taking the best footage he could get. She couldn't wait to watch it again later, maybe even tonight.

"You ready for us, now?" Jackson asked, eager to get inside Tessa. "You ready to get fucked by three big cocks all at once?"

Tessa moaned out, nodding at such a quick pace. "Yes," she gasped. "Fuck me, Jackson. Fuck me, Mike. Fuck me hard." The guys didn't really have much of a chance, though. Ben was occupying so much space on top of her. So instead, Tessa stroked their dicks while Ben railed her. Her screams only grew as her thoughts got filthier and filthier.

The room was filled with the cries of pleasure. Each man wanted Tessa to himself. Of course, that wasn't the plan. They'd all be sharing their time with her tonight.

Soon, the other guys couldn't wait anymore. They insisted Ben stop for a moment, and they repositioned her. Doggy style seemed to make the most sense. Mike got underneath her, so she could ride him. Jackson went to her face, gently playing with her hair as he positioned himself to be sucked. And behind her, Ben spat on his cock. It was already wet from being inside her. Between that and the spit, he figured he was probably lubed up enough to slide right into her ass. She was practically begging for it.

Soon, the men took her. They all slid into her gently, one after another. They grabbed at her, squeezing firmly. Her hair, her breasts, her hips, her ass. Each one pulled in his direction. She'd never felt so wanted. She did her best to please them all, but this was proving more difficult than the scenes she'd seen in porn.

"You like that, don't you?" Ben growled as they began to fuck her faster. "You like getting fucked by three big cocks. You like getting fucked while Kieran watches?"

Tessa groaned onto Jackson's cock. But her mouth was full. She tried to say yes. But she could only moan in response.

She managed to look up for a moment and get a glimpse of Kieran's eyes while he filmed her. She loved that her man was capturing all of this. She could tell he wanted to hear more from her. So she pulled back slightly and gasped for breath "I love it! Fuck me harder, guys! Use me all you want. Make me cum on your cocks!"

This was what all the men wanted to hear. Kieran loved it, feeling himself growing even harder. But he could only blush. Ben, Jackson, and Mike grinned, as they began to use her more thoroughly. The bed creaked loudly beneath them, the springs groaning with each hard thrust and bounce. It honestly sounded like they might shatter the entire bed frame. But nobody stopped, and none of the men were even willing to slow down. They were each chasing their own respective climaxes.

"I'm going to cum," Tessa gasped, her voice high and breathy. "Please boys, please, make me cum!"

Ben, Jackson, and Mike responded with growls and grunts, as each man was getting close, too. Finally, Tessa couldn't contain herself. She burst out screaming, and this caused the two guys still inside her to begin to cum. They all groaned loudly, almost in perfect unison

"Fuck!!!" Tessa cried out as Mike played with her nipples. She was filled with cum during one of the most intense orgasms of her life. She could do nothing else but scream.

Once she could handle it, she went back to sucking Jackson, although she was still experiencing smaller waves of her own climax. She sucked him good. Deep and fast. She wanted to give him an opportunity to experience his own release. And she did. Soon he yelled out, as if he were surprised out of nowhere.

"Oh! Oh! Oh God!!!" Jackson cried out. He pulled out of her mouth and finished on her face. Tessa could only feel pride from this. All the men made a mess of her. Mike in her pussy, Ben all over her back and ass, and Jackson on her face. Jackson continued stroking himself to get as much out as he could. Tessa took it as a compliment.

As they came back to Earth from their climaxes, Tessa couldn't help but giggle. She loved being covered in their mess. And she loved even more that Kieran had caught all of it on film.

The three of them lay together, basking in the afterglow of their session, as they all caught their breath. They were each ready to go another round. But this time, Kieran wanted in.

CHAPTER 8: ONE MORE GO

Tessa's body was still trembling from her climax, her skin slick with sweat as she lay on the bed, surrounded by Ben, Jackson, and Mike. But they weren't done with her yet. They wanted more, and Tessa was more than willing to give it to them.

Kieran, watching from the sidelines, felt his heart racing as he had watched his wife being taken by three men at once. He knew he should feel jealous, but all he felt was a deep, primal desire to join in, to be a part of the incredible passion that was unfolding before him.

Ben, Jackson, and Mike were still hard, their cocks glistening with Tessa's juices as they looked at each other, grinning. They knew what they wanted to do next.

Jackson lay down on the bed, his cock standing tall and proud as he pulled Tessa on top of him. She groaned as she was pulled atop him, and soon their passion reignited. She felt his big cock stretching her out, as he took what he wanted from underneath her. Ben and Mike positioned themselves on either side of her, stroking themselves as they considered what to do next.

Tessa sighed with pleasure as she felt their fingers trailing over her body. She knew what was coming, and she couldn't wait for round two.

Kieran, unable to resist any longer, walked right over and

joined them on the bed. Tessa's eyes widened, her face beaming with excitement as she saw her husband's cock, hard and throbbing, standing up straight and bobbing with each step. She wanted her man so badly.

Kieran positioned himself in front of Tessa, his fingers first, and then his cock rubbing against her lips. She moaned, bucking against Jackson as she felt Kieran's fingers trailing over her face. She could hardly wait for more attention.

"Ready for me, baby?" Kieran asked, unable to contain his pleasure. "You ready to see how much you can take?"

Tessa groaned with pleasure and nodded rapidly. This was all she'd ever wanted. "Yes!" she gasped loudly. "Fuck my mouth, Kieran. Fuck it however you like!"

Kieran grinned wide, not needing any more encouragement. Tessa groaned, her hips bouncing against Jackson's beneath her, as she felt Kieran's massive cock fill her mouth. Her man felt so big, so hard, and she knew she was going to get the fucking of her life. This was a dream come true.

It wasn't long before the other men wanted to reposition her. She didn't have enough openings, so they'd have to share. They began to each take one of them, and take turns rotating her and passing her around. And Tessa was a good girl. She took *everything* they gave her. The room was filled with the sounds of their passion; the slapping of flesh, groans, and muffled cries. It was a beautiful, chaotic symphony.

"You like that, honey?" Kieran smirked as she sucked him again. She loved being down on her knees, looking up at him. And she knew how much Kieran loved her eye contact.

Tessa moaned, moving her face back and forth to suck her man. She pulled back for a moment. "Yes," she said as she gasped for breath. "I love it! More, fuck me more!" she begged. Each guy was eager to please her.

The men continued their thrusting. Tonight's gangbang was going just as they'd all dreamed. Nobody had ever been part of one before. And they'd all been a bit nervous. But now, in this second round, they were all feeling like seasoned pros. Their thrusts, screams, spanks, and involuntary sounds of pleasure were all *so* hot.

"I'm going to cum," she gasped, Tessa's voice shakey. "Please! Please!!! Please make me cum again!!!"

And sure enough, they did. The boys took turns plunging themselves inside her. From every side, and every angle. Again and again, until she cried out and shook with pleasure.

And it didn't take long either, until all the men started to shoot their loads. All over Tessa. On her face, in her hair, on her ass, her back, and even a little bit in her mouth.

Tessa looked at Kieran, her eyes sparkling with love and desire. She was a mess. Just as she wanted to be.

She knew that this was just the beginning of a long, incredible journey together. But tonight was a great start.

It was literally a dream come true. Her Christmas miracle.

CHAPTER 9: CLEANING UP

The room was silent now, save for the rhythmic ticking of the clock on the wall and the occasional heavy breath as everyone came down from the night's incredible high. Tessa lay sprawled on the bed, her body still tingling from pleasure. Her skin was soaked with sweat and streaked with the evidence of her wildest fantasy, now fulfilled. She looked around at the smiling, satisfied faces of the men, her cheeks glowing with a mixture of embarrassment and pride.

Kieran leaned over her, brushing damp strands of hair from her face. "You good, love?" he asked softly, his voice full of affection and awe.

Tessa turned to him, her lips curling into a euphoric smile. "I've never been better. That was... everything I dreamed of and more." Her voice trembled slightly, still breathless from the intensity of the night.

Jackson, who was already half-dressed, chuckled as he pulled on his shirt. "Glad we could help make your dreams come true," he said, winking at Tessa.

"Definitely a night to remember," Mike added as he tossed his jacket over his shoulder. "Thanks for letting us be a part of it. You guys are... one hell of a couple."

Ben, still lounging on the edge of the bed, smirked. "And hey, if you ever need an encore…"

Tessa laughed, her eyes twinkling. "Don't tempt me. You might find yourselves invited back sooner than you think." Kieran blushed as he heard those words. He now knew for certain: Tessa had been *very* into this.

The men exchanged amused glances, clearly pleased with the idea. But as much as they'd all enjoyed themselves, the night had to come to an end. One by one, they said their goodbyes, leaving Tessa and Kieran alone in their bedroom.

When the door clicked shut behind the last guest, Tessa let out a giddy laugh and flopped back onto the bed. "Holy shit, Kieran. We actually did it."

Kieran climbed in beside her, pulling her into his arms. "We did," he said, kissing her forehead. "And you were amazing. You looked like you were in your element."

"I was," she admitted, her voice softening. "But I couldn't have done it without you. Knowing you were there, watching me, loving me, capturing everything—it made it perfect."

Kieran smiled, his hand tracing lazy circles on her back. "I love you, Tessa. I love that you trust me enough to share something like this. Tonight wasn't just about the fantasy—it was about us. About how strong we are together."

Tessa's eyes filled with tears—not of sadness, but of overwhelming joy. "I love you too, Kieran. So much. And you're right. This... this wasn't just about sex. It was about us exploring, growing, and living fully in the moment."

The couple lay there for a while, basking in the weight of the moment. Eventually, Tessa groaned and sat up, looking around the room. The bed was a mess, the sheets tangled and damp, and there were empty glasses and bottles scattered across the bedside tables.

"We should probably clean up," she said with a laugh.

Kieran grinned, grabbing his phone from the nightstand. "Not before we watch some of this footage."

Tessa's eyes widened, her cheeks flushing pink. "You're impossible," she said, swatting at him playfully. She didn't reveal it, but she genuinely loved this idea.

"Impossible, but yours," Kieran said, leaning in to kiss her deeply.

After a quick review of the highlights—both agreeing it was the hottest thing they'd ever seen—they got up and began tidying the room together. Laughter filled the space as they joked about the night, occasionally pausing to steal kisses or exchange teasing remarks.

When everything was back in order, they crawled into bed, pulling the fresh sheets over them. Tessa nestled against Kieran's chest, feeling safe, loved, and completely satisfied.

"So," Kieran murmured, stroking her hair. "What's next on that fantasy list of yours?"

Tessa grinned against his chest. "Oh, I've got plenty of ideas. But for now... I just want to fall asleep in your arms."

Kieran kissed the top of her head. "Sounds perfect to me."

And as the soft glow of the Christmas lights outside their window illuminated the room, the couple drifted off, holding each other close, content in the knowledge that they'd just experienced something truly unforgettable.

It had been a Christmas miracle indeed—and the beginning of an even deeper, more adventurous chapter in their love story.

If you enjoyed this story, please consider leaving a review! It

really helps small artists and creators like me better understand my customers. I sincerely appreciate your time reading this book, and humbly ask you for an honest review. Thank you <3

-Ms Naughtee

BOOKS BY THIS AUTHOR

Gangbang: At The Art Studio

In "Gangbang: At The Art Studio," prepare to be seduced by an uninhibited tale of unbridled passion and desire, as Luna and Jax invite five of Jax's closest friends to join them in an explosive night of unbridled pleasure within the intimate confines of their art studio.

Luna, a woman with an insatiable appetite for exploration, embarks on a thrilling sexual adventure that pushes the boundaries of her relationship with Jax. As their trusted circle of friends gathers, the group sets out to create a sensual masterpiece, their bodies merging in an erotic display of lust and devotion.

With each pulse-pounding moment, Luna surrenders herself to the skilled hands and mouths of her lovers, discovering new heights of ecstasy as she is worshipped and adored in every way imaginable. The art studio transforms into a playground of desire, the canvas beneath them bearing witness to the intensity of their passion.

"Gangbang: At The Art Studio" is a scorching hot and explicit tale that will leave readers breathless, yearning for more with every steamy encounter. This exhilarating story of trust, love, and unbridled desire will forever be seared into the minds of those who dare to indulge in its passionate pages.

Gangbang: A First Time For Everything

Join Jemma and her partner on a journey of exploration that transcends the boundaries of the ordinary. Playful spankings morph into something far more primal, and the lines between discipline and pleasure deliciously blur.

Dive into a world where playful teasing ignites a fire that can only be quenched by complete surrender.

But be warned, this story is not for the faint of heart. Prepare to be seduced by a rollercoaster ride of emotions, where naughty students discover the true meaning of punishment, and the lines between control and submission become beautifully blurred.

Please note: This book contains mature content and is intended for readers 18+

The Threesome: Mmf

In a long-term relationship that's grown comfortable but predictable, Katie surprises her boyfriend with a proposition: explore their desires together, with the inclusion of their friend Brandon. This unexpected invitation sparks a whirlwind of conversations about intimacy, honesty, and the boundaries of love. As they navigate uncharted territory together, they discover that communication and trust are the foundation for any relationship, even a non-traditional one. Will their exploration lead to disaster, or ignite a deeper connection? Dive into this story of unexpected desires, open communication, and the courage to explore new possibilities.

Made in the USA
Monee, IL
22 May 2025

17888430R00024